Disney
MICKEY & FRIENDS

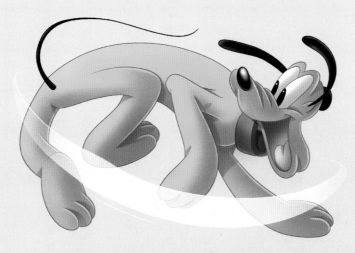

This special edition was printed for Kohl's Department Stores, Inc. (for distribution on behalf of Kohl's Cares, LLC, its wholly owned subsidiary), by Disney Press, New York/Los Angeles.

Kohl's
1204045-00
123387
07/14–08/14

Printed in China
First Edition
1 3 5 7 9 10 8 6 4 2
ISBN 978-1-4847-2161-2
G615-7693-2-14182

For more Disney Press fun, visit www.disneybooks.com

Disney PRESS
New York • Los Angeles

One sunny morning, Mickey Mouse looked out the window. "What a beautiful day!" he exclaimed.

His nephews, Ferdie and Morty, joined him.

"Can we go play outside, Uncle Mickey?" Morty asked.

"Yeah!" said Ferdie. "We can play with Pluto in the yard!"

While Mickey stayed inside to clean up after breakfast, Morty and Ferdie happily went outside with Pluto.

"Let's teach him to do tricks," said Ferdie.

"Roll over, Pluto," said Morty.

But Pluto just sat up and begged.

"Hmmm. That didn't work," said Morty.

"Maybe we should show him what to do," said Ferdie.

The boys began to roll around on the ground. "Like this, Pluto," they said. But Pluto just watched them, confused.

"Let's try something *he* likes to do," said Morty.
Ferdie threw a stick for Pluto. "Fetch!" he said.
But instead of fetching, Pluto jumped up and began to chase his tail.

"It looks like Pluto has a little too much energy for the yard," Mickey said, joining the boys. "Why don't you take him to the park?"

Mickey paused. "Besides," he added. "I think today is more of a *building* day than a *cleaning* day!"

"What are you going to build, Uncle Mickey?" said Ferdie.

Mickey's eyes twinkled. "Oh, I don't know," he said. "Maybe . . . a tree house!"

Morty and Ferdie jumped up and down. "A tree house?" Ferdie said.

"Can we help?" Morty asked.

"You would be great helpers," Mickey replied. "But there will be lots of tools in the yard. It might not be very safe. I think you'll be safer spending the afternoon at the park."

Morty and Ferdie reluctantly agreed and, after putting on Pluto's leash, raced off down the sidewalk.

With Morty, Ferdie, and Pluto gone, Mickey called his friends. He told them all about the tree house and asked if they would like to help.

Mickey's friends were more than happy to help. They were excited about such a fun project and agreed to meet at Mickey's house.

● ● ● ● ● ● ● ● ● ●

Mickey was waiting by his gate when Minnie arrived.

"Oh, Mickey, I'm so excited," she said. "This will be so much fun! Just wait until you see the idea I had."

"Building a tree house is a big job," Mickey said when the rest of his friends arrived. "Maybe we should split up the work."

"Great idea, Mickey!" said Goofy.

"Why don't you saw the boards, Goofy," Mickey said. "Then Donald and I can hammer them together."

Minnie showed Mickey her idea.

"Good thinking, Minnie!" Mickey replied. "That will be one of the most important jobs."

Goofy dumped out his toolbox in a corner of the yard. The tools made a big *crash*—and a big mess! Goofy found what he was looking for and began sawing the boards.

After a few minutes, Minnie walked up to him. "Sorry to bother you, Goofy," she began. "I was wondering if you would cut some boards for me, too?"

"Sure!" Goofy said with a grin. "Just tell me what you need."

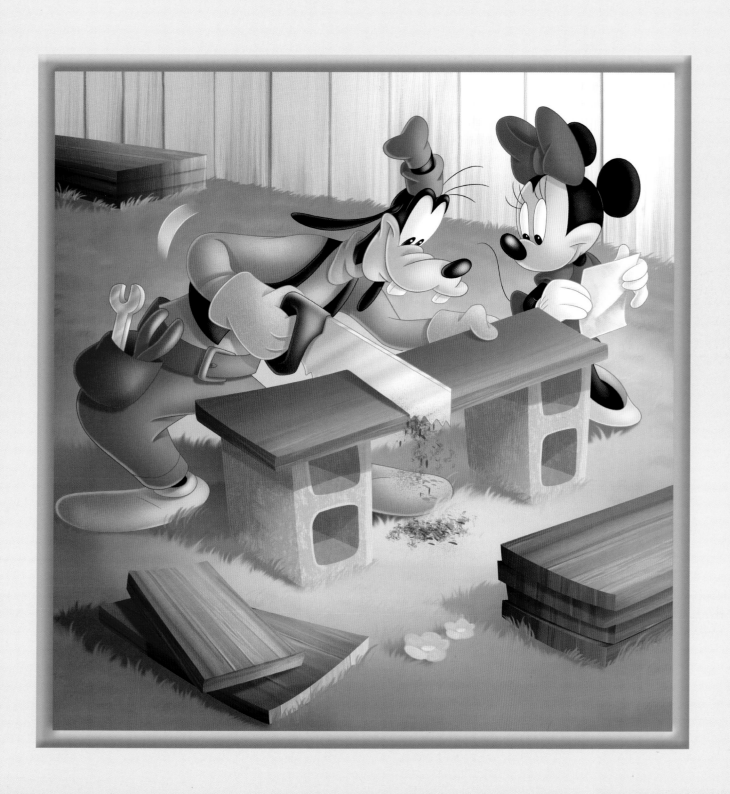

Over by the big tree, Donald and Mickey worked together to make a rope ladder. When they were finished, Mickey attached the ladder to the thickest branch. He gave the ladder a strong tug. It didn't budge.

"That should do it," Mickey said. "Once we finish building, we can use this ladder to climb into the tree house."

Just then, Goofy brought them a stack of boards. "Here you go!" he said proudly. "I still have to saw the boards for the roof, but you can use these for the floor and the walls."

"Thanks, Goofy!" Mickey said.

Mickey and Donald climbed into the tree, pulling the boards behind them. The sound of their hammers echoed through the backyard as Mickey and Donald started building.

Across the yard, Minnie pulled her hammer out of her tool belt. As she picked up the first board, she realized that she had forgotten something very important.

Minnie hurried over to the big tree. "Do you have any extra nails?" she called up. "I left all of mine at home!"

"I have some," Donald said. He fished a box of nails out of his tool belt and gave them to Minnie.

On the way back to her project, Minnie stopped to see how Daisy was doing.

"Wow, Daisy," Minnie said. "You mixed up a lot of paint!"

Daisy giggled. "I might have mixed a little *too* much," she said. "Do you need any paint for your project?"

"Thanks, Daisy," Minnie said. "That would be great!"

• • • • • • • • • •

Buzz-buzz-buzz went the saw.
Bang-bang-bang went the hammers.
Swish-swish-swish went the paintbrushes.
Mickey's backyard was a very busy place!

Later that day, Morty, Ferdie, and Pluto came home from the park. Morty and Ferdie couldn't believe their eyes. "Wow!" the boys cried.

"That's the best tree house ever!" added Ferdie. Then they scrambled up the rope ladder.

But Pluto stayed behind. He tilted his head and stared at the ladder. He couldn't climb it like the others.

Mickey understood right away. "Don't worry, Pluto!" he called. "Come around to the other side of the tree."

Pluto trotted around the tree and found something that made his tail wag: a set of stairs that was just his size!

"Minnie made them for you," Mickey explained. "Now come on up and join the fun!"

Pluto ran up the stairs. It really was the best tree house ever!